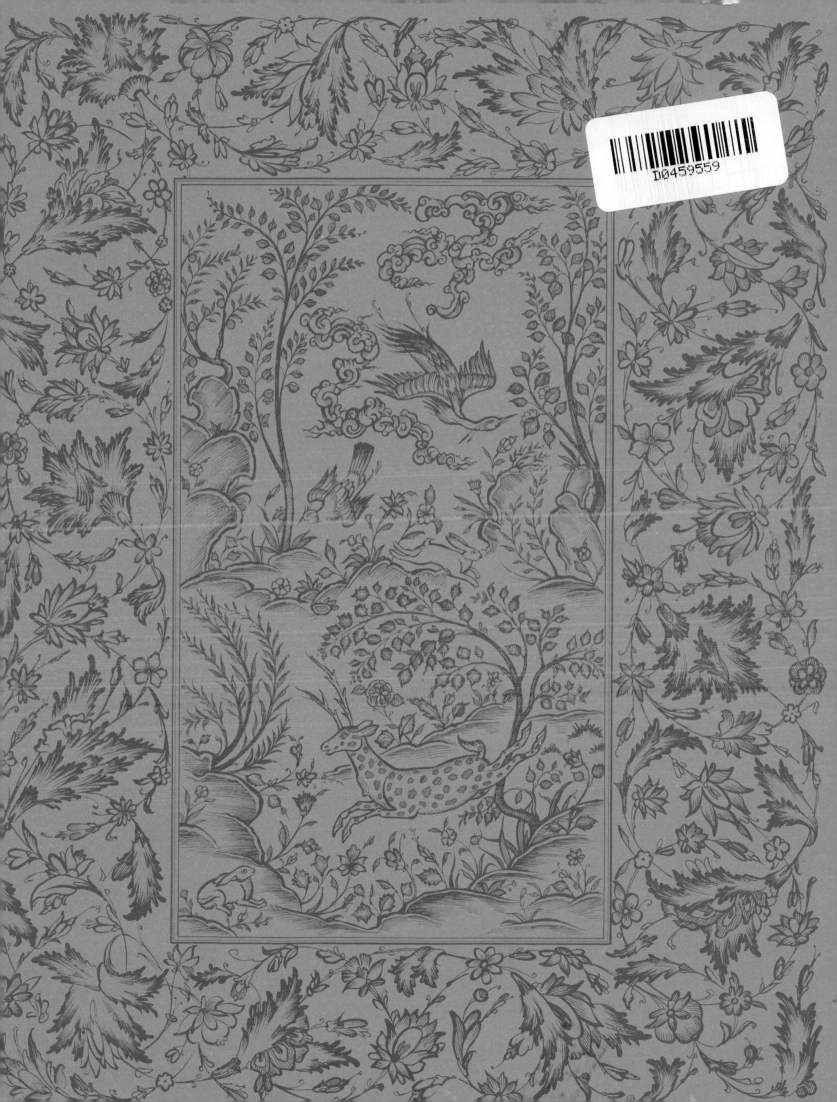

Illustrated by Laurel Long

The Lady & the Lion

A Brothers Grimm tale retold by Laurel Long & Jacqueline K. Ogburn

Dial Books · New York

Published by Dial Books for Young Readers
A division of Penguin Young Readers Group
345 Hudson Street
New York, New York 10014

Designed by Nancy R. Leo-Kelly
Text set in Perpetua
Manufactured in China on acid-free paper
1 3 5 7 9 10 8 6 4 2

Library of Congress Cataloging-in-Publication Data
Long, Laurel.
The lady and the lion / by Laurel Long and Jacqueline K. Ogburn ;
illustrated by Laurel Long.
p.   cm.
Summary: With help from Sun, Moon, and North Wind, a lady travels
the world seeking to save her beloved from the evil enchantress who
turned him first into a lion, then into a dove.
ISBN 0-8037-2651-1
[1. Fairy tales. 2. Folklore—Germany.]
I. Title: Lady and the lion. II. Ogburn, Jacqueline K. III. Title.
PZ8.L848 Lad 2003   398.2—dc21   2002004007

The art for this book was created using oil paints on watercolor paper.

Authors' Note

This Grimms' fairy tale is also known as "The Singing, Springing Lark."
It is an Aarne-Thompson tale type 425, "the search for the lost husband,"
a type that also includes animal bridegroom tales. The story combines
"Beauty and the Beast" and "East of the Sun, West of the Moon." Our retelling
condenses the action, but we chose to follow the dramatic spirit of the ending
of "East of the Sun, West of the Moon" in our treatment of the villain.

For Shea —L.L.

To my family: Ben, Claire, and Emily —J.K.O.

Once upon a time, a merchant asked his three daughters what he should bring them from the city. The first asked for pearls, the second for gold, but the youngest longed for a singing lark. The merchant found a pearl necklace and a bracelet of gold, but there were no songbirds to be had for love or money that winter.

He turned toward home, sorry to disappoint his youngest daughter. The road took him past a fine castle, with a grand garden full of spring flowers in spite of the winter snows. At the top of a laurel tree, a lark sang.

The merchant climbed the tree and had just captured the lark, when a loud roar split the air. "I eat those who steal from me," said a great lion, standing below.

"I did not know the bird was yours," said the merchant. "Please, spare me."

"Promise me whatever first greets you when you return home. Then you may have your life and my bird," said the lion.

The merchant hesitated, because his youngest daughter was often the first to greet him. The lion growled with impatience, shaking the leaves. The merchant also shook at the idea of staying trapped in the tree. He thought, Perhaps it will only be my hunting dog or the barn cat. So he agreed to the bargain.

When the merchant neared home, his heart sank to see his youngest daughter running toward him. "I have your singing lark, but at too high a cost," he said. He told of the fierce lion and his promise. "I cannot let you go, for the lion will tear you to pieces."

But his daughter said, "Dear Father, you taught us to keep our word. I will go to the lion and perhaps he will free me too."

The next morning she set out into the forest with the singing lark and a brave heart. She arrived at dusk to find the great lion standing at the castle gate. A dozen more lions came and took their places, watching her with their golden eyes. The great lion circled around her, then stopped in front of her and waited.

"I have come to keep my father's promise. A lion that loves birds will do no harm," she said, handing him the lark. She showed no fear, but her knees trembled. Her words and courage touched the lion's heart.

"Welcome to my home, lady," the great lion said. The lady looked into his gentle eyes and became less afraid.

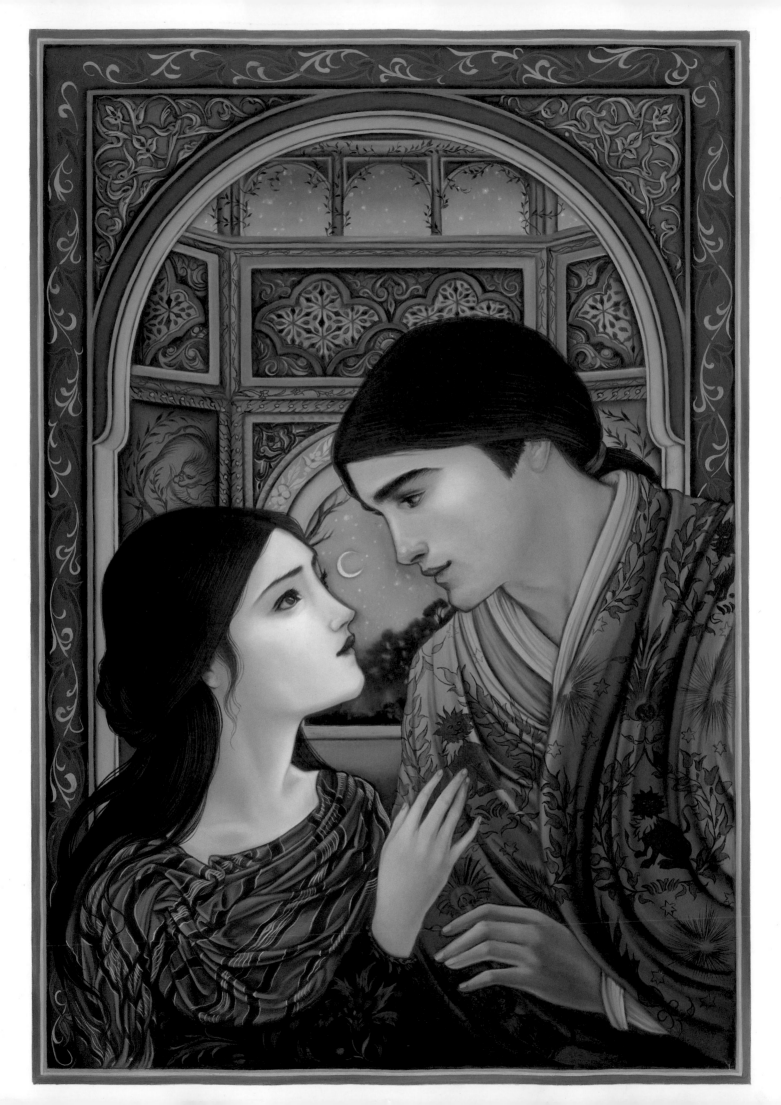

He led her inside the castle. The only light came from the last rays of the setting sun visible through the window. She turned to speak, then gasped. Next to her stood not the lion, but a handsome young man.

"Please, do not be afraid," he said, looking at her with the lion's eyes. "A wicked enchantress cast a spell on me when I refused to marry her. My court and I are lions by day and humans by night. Stay with us."

"I will keep my father's promise, whether you are human or lion," said the lady. "Light a candle so I can see you clearly."

"I dare not," he replied. "This curse has another part. If a ray of candlelight touches me, I become a white dove, forced to fly across the world for seven years."

So the lady stayed with the lion. They soon grew to love each other, for the prince was as gentle and kind in his human form as he was strong in his lion form. They married and lived happily. Together they planted a garden full of night-blooming flowers.

At times they would roam through the woods in the daylight, with the lady riding upon the lion's back. She still loved songbirds, and the lion knew just where to find the ones that sang most sweetly.

One day news came that her sisters were to be married. The lady longed to see her family again and introduce her beloved husband.

The prince offered to have his lions escort her. "Please, come with me," she said to him. Unable to deny his lady anything, the prince agreed and they set out the next day.

Her family was delighted to see her. The lady had a room built in her father's house, with walls so thick, no light could penetrate. As night fell, the lion shut himself inside. But the wood of the door was green, and as it dried, a tiny crack appeared.

After the church ceremony, the wedding party returned to the merchant's house, carrying candles to light their way. As the procession came into the house past the darkened room, a splinter of candlelight no wider than a hair pierced the door and touched the prince. When the lady opened the door, she gasped to see only a white dove huddled inside.

The dove said, "For seven years I must fly across the wide world. Every seventh step you take, I will drop a white feather to guide you. If you follow, we can be together again." The dove flew over her head and out the door, dropping a feather as he did so. The lady caught the feather and followed.

On she ran, looking neither right nor left, nor stopping to rest. Near the end of the seven years, she rejoiced, thinking they would soon be together. But suddenly there was no feather to guide her. When she looked up, the white dove had vanished.

Desperate, she turned her face to the sky. "Sun, you shine in every valley and on every mountaintop. Have you seen my white dove?"

"I have not seen your dove," said the sun. "But I give you this chest to open in your hour of need." The lady thanked the sun and traveled on until night.

eary, she rested at the edge of a woodland stream. She looked up at the full moon and said, "Moon, you shine over every field and every forest. Have you seen my white dove?"

A ribbon of moonlight washed the palm of her hand with a burst of blue light. As the light faded, she held what looked like a common hen's egg.

"I have not seen your dove," said the moon. "But I give you this egg to break open in your hour of need." She thanked the moon and walked on.

At the edge of the wild wood the earth dropped down to the sea. The lady stopped. She said, "North Wind, you blow through every leaf and flower. Have you seen my white dove?"

Suddenly a blast of wind came with such force that she feared being blown off the cliff onto the rocks below. "I have seen your dove," whispered the North Wind. "In his lion form he fights a dragon by the Red Sea. This dragon is also the enchantress who cursed him. He needs your help. Ride my griffin there and distract the dragon so the lion may overcome her. When the dragon falls, they will both return to human form. Take your husband onto the griffin at once. Do not delay, or you will not escape her."

The lady thanked the North Wind. She flew the griffin to the Red Sea, where she saw her lion battling the dragon. Frightened, the lady urged the griffin to fly straight at the dragon's face. The dragon snapped viciously at the griffin. The lion saw his chance and pounced. He drove his teeth and claws into the dragon's neck, and they went crashing to the surf.

Lying stunned at the edge of the shore, they both became human again. In her joy, the lady forgot the North Wind's warning. Instead, she jumped off the griffin and ran to her husband.

While they embraced, the enchantress mounted the griffin. Swooping down upon them, she ripped the prince away and flew with him across the wide sea.

The lady, angry over forgetting the North Wind's advice, sat by the water's edge and wept. At last she dried her eyes and vowed, "As long as the sun shines and the moon glows, I will search until I find him."

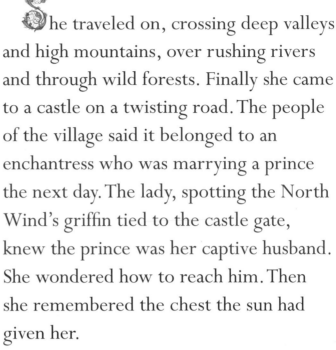

She traveled on, crossing deep valleys and high mountains, over rushing rivers and through wild forests. Finally she came to a castle on a twisting road. The people of the village said it belonged to an enchantress who was marrying a prince the next day. The lady, spotting the North Wind's griffin tied to the castle gate, knew the prince was her captive husband. She wondered how to reach him. Then she remembered the chest the sun had given her.

Opening the chest, she found a golden dress spun from sunlight and as brilliant as the day. The lady put it on and walked into the castle with her head held high. She was met by the enchantress, who was dazzled by the bright beauty of the dress. The enchantress said, "In that gown I would outshine the sun. I must have it for my wedding. What will you take for it?"

The lady replied, "I have heard so much about the courage of your prince. Let me meet him and I will give you the dress." The enchantress did not like this, but she so longed for the dress that she agreed. Then she ordered her servant to sneak a sleeping potion into the prince's drink.

The lady was led into the tower where her prince was a prisoner in a room with one window facing the sea. When she arrived, he was asleep. The lady tried to shake him awake, but he slept on. Despondent, she sat by his side and said, "For seven years I followed you across the wide world. I asked the sun and the moon and the North Wind for news of you. When you fought the dragon, I helped you. Please, wake up now!" But to the prince, her cries seemed to be the wind rustling through the trees.

Then the lady remembered the moon's egg. She cracked it open. Inside she found a silver cup, edged with pearls and filled with liquid. She raised the cup to the prince's lips and poured the liquid into his mouth. He opened his eyes and said, "I dreamed we were together again."

While the lady and the prince rejoiced, the brilliant sun dress turned into soot in the enchantress's hands. Enraged, she rushed up the tower stairs. Hearing her footsteps, the lady and the prince ran to the window. "There is no escape," said the prince. "I will have to fight again."

But the lady had another idea. "North Wind!" she cried. "Unleash your griffin so we may be carried home!"

The tower door burst open and the enchantress charged the lovers just as the griffin reached the window. Quickly they jumped onto the griffin's back. The enchantress lunged at them. Losing her balance, she fell headfirst out the window and crashed upon the rocks below, never to cause trouble again.

Into the light of the new day, the lady and her prince
flew on the griffin across the wide world to
their home where the flowers
bloomed all year long.
And they lived happily
forever after.